LEARN TO R

LAURA LEE
and the
Monster Sea

by Alice Sullivan Finlay
illustrated by Julie Durrell

ZondervanPublishingHouse

Grand Rapids, Michigan

A Division of HarperCollinsPublishers

Laura Lee and the Monster Sea
Text copyright © 1993 by Alice Sullivan Finlay
Illustration copyright © 1993 by Julie Durrell

Requests for information should be addressed to:
Zondervan Publishing House
Grand Rapids, Michigan 49530

Library of Congress Cataloging-in-Publication Data

Finlay, Alice Sullivan.
    Laura Lee and the monster sea / Alice Sullivan Finlay.
        p. cm.
    Summary: While vacationing with her family at the beach, Laura Lee
prays that God's love will help her overcome her fear of the monster
sea.
    ISBN 0-310-59841-9 (pbk.)
    [1. Beaches—Fiction. 2. Fear—Fiction. 3. Vacations—Fiction
4. Christian life—Fiction.] I. Title.
PZ7.F49579Lau   1993
[E]–dc20   93-3500
                                                          CIP
                                                          AC

Edited by Dave Lambert and Leslie Kimmelman
Interior and cover design by Steven M. Scott
Illustrations by Julie Durrell

Printed in the United States of America

93 94 95 96 97 98 / CH / 10 9 8 7 6 5 4 3 2 1

To my mom and dad,
Alice and Tim Sullivan,
for seashore memories.

CHAPTER ONE

"I want to go home,"
said Laura Lee.
Waves lapped at her feet
like a giant cat.
Her foot sank.
Her brother Randy
chased her with a clam.
"Get away from me," said Laura Lee.
"Something grabbed my feet."
"It was only seaweed," said Randy.
"Don't be a baby."

Laura Lee ran to her mom and dad.

The ocean roared in her ears.

"There is a monster in the sea,"
she said.

Her father held her hand.

"You will learn to like it here,"
he said.

"No, not me," said Laura Lee.

They walked to their house.

Her brother raced inside.

"I love it here!" he shouted.

Laura Lee sniffed.

"How long are we staying?"
she asked.

"Two weeks," said Mom.

Laura Lee frowned.

Why can't I be more like Randy?

she thought.

He was never afraid.

He made a funny face at her,

and she laughed.

"See? You will have fun here,"

said Randy.

"No, not me," said Laura Lee.

After dinner,

the family watched the sun set.

Dad took out his Bible.

"Perfect love drives out fear,"

he read.

"Do you know what that means?"

he asked Laura Lee.

Laura Lee shook her head.

"God's love is perfect," Dad said.

"Trust him.

Soon you won't be afraid here."

Dad carried Laura Lee piggyback

to her room.

Moonlight beamed in.

"The moon is God's night-light,"

he said.

He kissed her good night.

Laura Lee yawned.

Tomorrow she would try

to have a better day.

CHAPTER TWO

In the morning, Randy shook her.

"Let's go," he said.

"I'm going to catch the biggest crab
in the sea.

Do you want one too, Sis?"

"No, not me," said Laura Lee.

But she remembered what her dad
had said.

Perfect love drives out fear.

She would go with Randy
and try to have fun.

They ran along the beach to the docks.

Randy put down his bucket.

He pointed to the crabs.

"I love creepy, crawly things.

Don't you, Sis?"

"No, not me," said Laura Lee.

Randy bought some gooey squid

from the bait man.

Laura Lee wrinkled her nose at it.

"Crabs like this," Randy said.

"Even if you don't."

He baited a hook.

He dropped the hook into the water.

A crab grabbed it with its claw.

But when Randy pulled the string,

the crab let go.

Randy tried again and again.

11

"You try, Sis," he said.

"All right," Laura Lee said slowly.

She dropped the string

into the water.

"You have one!" Randy squealed.

She pulled up a spotted crab.

"Good job, Sis," he said.

"He will be a nice pet."

Laura Lee filled the bucket

with sand and water.

Randy put the crab into the bucket.

"He is ugly," Laura Lee said.

"Catch another crab, Sis,"

said Randy.

"Then we can have crab races."

"No, not me," said Laura Lee.

CHAPTER THREE

The next day,
sunlight danced on the bay.
Laura Lee watched the sailboats.
Maybe I will like it here,
she thought.

"Let's go to the beach,"
said her dad.
They carried chairs and towels.
Laura Lee wiggled her toes
in the warm sand.
Sea gulls dove for clams
"I'm going to ride the biggest wave,"
said Randy.
Laura Lee stared at
the monster sea.
Her dad patted her shoulder.
"Are you ready to learn to swim?"
he asked.
"No, not me," said Laura Lee.
"I will hold you tight,"
her father said. "I promise."
"Well, all right," Laura Lee said.

Randy splashed into the ocean.
Laura Lee's dad carried her
piggyback above the waves.
Mom waded beside them.

Laura Lee looked at the waves.

They were big, and they were loud.

She was afraid.

Her dad and mom held her

over the water.

She rocked in the monster sea.

She tried to pray,

but she was still afraid.

She grabbed on tight.

"Take me in, Daddy," she said.

He set her on the beach.

Foamy waves splashed her feet.

She shivered.

"We will try again later,"

said her dad.

"No, not me," said Laura Lee.

Randy played with his crab
in a sand fort.

"He looks sick," Laura Lee said.

"He is all right," said Randy.

Poor crab, she thought.
He is just like me.
He does not like to be away
from home either.

At lunch, her father smiled.

"Tomorrow we will rent a boat,"
he said. "Are you ready
for the high seas, sport?"

"No, not me," said Laura Lee.

CHAPTER FOUR

Laura Lee held on to her hat.
Her stomach flopped
when she stepped into the boat.
The boat looked small
on the giant monster sea.

"Does God know we are here?"

she asked.

"God knows everything,"

said her father.

She tied on a life jacket.

"Are you scared?" her mother asked.

"No, not me," said Laura Lee.

"Well—maybe a little."

The motor roared.

The boat pulled away from the docks.

Her dad let it drift in the bay.

"I will catch the biggest fish,"

said Randy.

Laura Lee dropped her line

into the water.

Randy caught two fish.

Laura Lee wished she could catch one.

There was a tug on her line.

"I have one!" she yelled.

"Oh, boy!" said Randy.

He jumped and rocked the boat.

"Steady now," said Laura Lee's father.

He helped her reel in the fish.

Her heart beat fast.

"It's pretty," she said.

"It's a giant flounder," said Randy.

"You can eat him for dinner,"
said her mom.

"No, not me," said Laura Lee.

Later, her dad cleaned the fish.

The family sat down to eat.

They thanked God for the food.

"Good job, Sis," said Randy.

Laura Lee smiled.

"Is this my fish?" she asked.

Her mother nodded.

Laura Lee took a big helping.

Her dad winked at her.

"I thought you did not like fish,"
he said.

"No, not me," said Laura Lee.

CHAPTER FIVE

The next day,

Laura Lee looked at the crab.

He was hardly moving.

What if he dies? she thought.

"What's wrong?" she asked the crab.

"I bet you are homesick,

just like I was.

I am taking you home right now."

She carried the bucket outside.

Randy stopped playing ball.

"What are you doing with my crab?"

he asked.

"We have to take him back
before he dies," she said.
"See? He is swimming on his side."
Randy frowned.
"I wanted to show my friends
back home," he said.
"But I don't want him to die.
Do you, Sis?"
"No, not me," said Laura Lee.

She carried the bucket
to the docks.
Randy stood by her side.
She turned the bucket over.
"He isn't moving," said Randy.
Laura Lee picked up the crab.
His claw pinched her finger.
"Ouch!" she said.
"He is alive."
She put the crab in the bay.
"You are home," she said.

The crab walked to the other crabs.

"He will be all right," Laura Lee said.

She rubbed her finger.

"I thought I could keep him forever," said Randy.

"Are you sad he's gone, Sis?"

"No, not me," said Laura Lee.

CHAPTER SIX

That night, Laura Lee prayed,
"Lord, the crab was brave
to live away from his home.
I want to be brave, too.
Please help me.
I want to be happy
here at the ocean.
I want to swim in the monster sea."

In the morning,
she knew what she would do.
Laura Lee ran downstairs
in her swimsuit.
"I want to learn to swim,"
she said.
Her dad smiled.
"Are you sure, sport?" he asked.
"Yes," she said.
"I know God will help me."
They went to the beach.
Dad carried Laura Lee
above the waves.
Her mother was by her side.

"You can do it, Sis!" yelled Randy.

Her father held her

over the water.

She relaxed in his strong arms.

Water rushed under her belly.

She licked salt from her lips.

"Move your arms," said Dad.

"Kick your feet," said Mom.

Laura Lee started to move.

Her dad let go.

"I'm swimming!" Laura Lee said.

"That's my girl," said Dad.

"We knew you could do it,"
said Mom.

"Yay, Sis!" yelled Randy.

She started to sink.

Her dad caught her.

"Did you have enough for today?"

he asked.

"No, not me," said Laura Lee.

She paddled and kicked.

The monster sea held her up.

"Thank you, God," she prayed,

"for helping me to be brave."

They went back to the beach.

"I did it!" she said.

"Soon I will ride the waves."

"Nice going, sport," said her dad.

"Are you still afraid of the sea?"
asked Randy.

"No, not me," said Laura Lee.

Walking home,

she looked for the crab.

They were all spotted.

But Laura Lee was sure she saw him.

"That's him," she said.

"I know it is."

"You saved his life," said Randy.

He picked up a clam and chased her.

She laughed.

"I'm not afraid," she said.

Her mother and father smiled.

She knew now that home

was anywhere her family was, and

that God's perfect love kept her safe.

"The crab is happy to be home,"
she said.
Her dad took her hand.
"I bet you will be glad
to go home, too," said Mom.
"No, not me," said Laura Lee.

The End

Did you enjoy this book about Laura Lee? I have good news—there are *more* Laura Lee books! Read about them on the following pages.

The Laura Lee books are available at your local Christian bookstore, or you can order direct from 800-727-3480.

Don't miss...

Zondervan Publishing House
0-310-59851-6

A Victory for Laura Lee

**The neighborhood pond
is full of trash...
and Laura Lee is angry.**

When Laura Lee visits the pond
near her house, she finds lots of
trash—and a very sick duck who
is choking on a piece of plastic.
Will the duck live? Can Laura Lee
and her friends clean up the pond
and keep it clean? Can they give
the animals a safe home?

Don't miss...

Zondervan Publishing House
0-310-59871-0

A Gift from the Sea for Laura Lee

**Laura Lee's friend Shona is rich...
but Laura Lee is not.**

When Laura Lee and her family visit her grandma at the seashore, Laura Lee meets Shona. But Shona says that her family is rich. Will Shona still like Laura Lee even though Laura Lee's family is not rich? Will Laura Lee tell Shona the truth? And who will win the fishing contest?

Laura Lee's dad and grandma help her solve a tough problem in *A Gift from the Sea for Laura Lee*.

Don't miss...

Zondervan Publishing House
0-310-59861-3

Laura Lee and the Little Pine Tree

**A cabin without lights, water...
or a bathroom?**

That's where Laura Lee and her family are spending the week, high in the mountains. Having to pump their own water and use an old out-house for a bathroom is bad enough. But who is stealing their food? Is it a bear? And why did it have to snow? And what can Laura Lee do when her brother Randy disappears?

"This is too much for me," says Laura Lee.